Amelia's
MIDDLE-SCHOOL
GRADUATION
Yearbook

by Marissa Moss

except for words and pictures by Amelia

Creston Books

Berkeley,
California

This book is dedicated to Sara and Olivia —
congratulations on graduating from middle school!

Copyright © 2015 by Marissa Moss
All rights reserved, including the right of reproduction
in whole or in part, in any way, shape, or form without
written permission from the publisher.
Amelia® and the notebook design
are registered trademarks of Marissa Moss.

Thanks,
Simon! → Book design by Amelia
(with help from Simon Stahl, designer)   And boy,
are my
The text for this book is hand-lettered. ←   hands
Manufactured in the U.S.A.   tired!
CIP data for this book is available
from the Library of Congress
2 4 6 8 10 9 7 5 3 1
ISBN: 978-1-939547-09-5

Creston Books
Berkeley,
California

Long, long ago, when I started middle school, I thought 8th graders were super scary.

How 8th graders looked to me when I was a lowly 6th grader. They seemed so grown-up and snotty. They even spoke their own language.

No way! · Way! · Way, way!

I felt like a tiny shrimp, dwarfed by my huge backpack. And hopelessly uncool.

When I started 8th grade myself, it was the first time I'd begun a new school year without worrying about looking like a dork. I remember that first day so clearly — Carly and I were on top of the world!

Carly and me as non-snotty 8th graders ↓

We were Rulers of the Halls, Kings of the Cafeteria! ↘

And now 8th grade is almost over. Which turns out to be even scarier than starting as a 6th grader. Because the end of 8th grade means the end of middle school.

Which means the start of high school.

Which is terrifying in so many ways, I don't want to think about it. Lucky for me I have a true friend I can count on, no matter what.

I remember the first time I saw Carly. I'd just moved to Oopa in the middle of 4th grade. So not only was I the new kid, I was joining the class part-way through— the worst way to start a new school!

I could tell Carly would be a great friend because she was so confident, smart, and funny. I just wanted to be around her.

We've been through a lot since 4th grade. We've fought and made up so many times, we really know how to be friends. In a way, we've grown up together, tried things and succeeded, tried things and failed.

Like when we wanted to make some money. Selling lemonade didn't work out so well. We ended up drinking it all since nobody bought any, which was a BIG mistake.

↓

lemon pucker →

way too full and squooshy →

FRESH COLD
LEMONADE
25¢ a cup
COME AND GET IT!

lemonade bloat—my pants were ready to explode!

↑
Nobody came and got it.

Since being practical didn't work (lemonade is very practical), we tried for dream jobs instead. ⟶

It looks like fun — and it is!

HOLIDAY WINDOW PAINTER

ICE CREAM TASTER
~ YUM. YUM ~

Hmmm, needs a touch more chocolate.

MOVIE REVIEWER

I give it a big thumbs-up! Good popcorn too!

CHILDREN'S BOOK
AUTHOR and ILLUSTRATOR

I get to write and draw all day!

↖ Which, of course, didn't work, either, but were a lot more fun to imagine.

We did finally figure out how to make money, but it was way more work than we thought it would be.

First we tried dog-care. ↓

WOOF WA[LKER]
No dog too big, no t[oo...]
Call Amelia or Ca[rly...]

WOOF WALKER

No dog too big, no bark too loud.
Call Amelia or Carly at →

Until one dog ran away and broke a window. →

Then we started a babysitting business, which we barely survived. I couldn't have done any of it without Carly! ↓

peanut butter in hair →

jelly on shirt ↓

bandage on foot →

← borrowed sweatpants

Plus she helped me survive middle school. From the evil teacher, Mr. Lambaste, in 6th grade...

One look from him could sour the whole day.

A glare from him ruined the whole week.

And if he actually said something – his usual

I had him for 2 classes – English and Social Studies – doubling the misery.

ugly insults – that was it for the month.

...to running for student council together.

Since Carly ran for president, we made most of the posters for her. I only ran for secretary to keep her company. My main job was poster-making. I didn't have to make any speeches, like she did (luckily!). I'd much rather draw than debate any day!

STUDENT TV
VOTE 4 CARLY!

It's not Picture Day.

Relax - Act natural!

STUDENT TV
VOTE 4 CARLY!

VOTE!

Vote!

I vote 4 Carly 4 everything!

... to school dances, science fairs, group projects, oral reports. Carly made all of it better.

So now, of course, Carly is planning on how to make the end of the year — the end of middle school — the best celebration ever. Starting with a big BBQ after graduation. It's going to be a lot more than a picnic. She has so many ideas, she brought a clipboard to school to keep track of things.

I don't know how Carly can think about food. All I can focus on is that these three years are over. And high school is about to start.

what can you bring? Leah's in charge of s'mores, Sacha's doing burgers.

I'll take care of reggie kebobs. So what else?

I should be savoring every last second of my top dog status, but I can't shut out the creeping worry of what back-to-the-bottom-AGAIN 9th grade will be like. Why is school like this, a constant climb to the top? First you trudge from kindergarten all the way to 5th grade. Then you're back at the bottom, climbing from 6th grade to 8th. Just when you reach the top, you plummet back down. To 9th grade, where you start all over again.

Until you reach 12th grade. When you start AGAIN as a college freshman.

Help! I'm falling!

KER-PLUNK!

Who designed school to work this way?

HIGH SCHOOL

WHAT'S SCARY

WHAT'S EXCITING— DARE I SAY, MAYBE EVE FUN?

WHAT'S SCARY	WHAT'S EXCITING
Being around older kids.	Being around older kids.
A new school, possibly getting lost, figuring out which teachers are good, which to avoid at all costs.	A clean slate, where no teac has heard anything about y
Grades suddenly REALLY matter.	Fun electives like Auto Sh and Computer Design.
P.E., uniforms, gyms, showers. (Ick! UGH!! GROSS!!!)	Not having to take P.E. ev year. FINALLY-YAAAY!
Boy friends?	Boy friends!
Learning to drive, maybe getting a ticket or denting the car.	Getting good at driving (assuming that happens, but looking at Mom, maybe not).

Besides all that, 9th grade means a whole new grouping of who's cool and who's not. Meaning more chances for embarrassment and social disasters.

YIKES!! The worst social nightmare is that I'll be in the same school as my sister, Cleo. There are a gazillion ways for her to make me look bad. Who doesn't know her ridiculous reputation?

Nobody! The whole school could ace this Cleo test:

① Cleo likes to stick French fries up her nose.
True ☐
False ☐

Is this some sort of bizarre experiment? I won't give you extra credit.

② Cleo once threw up on her science teacher, and he thought she did it on purpose.
True ☐
False ☐

③ Cleo once went to school wearing a nightgown as an English project, saying she was Lady MacBeth.

True ☐

False ☐

④ Cleo almost ran over a P.E. class when she took Mom's car for a practice drive in the school parking lot.

True ☐

False ☐

⑤ Cleo dressed up as a pop singer for the school talent show and sang "I Did It My Way."

True ☐

False ☐

⑥ For Cinco de Mayo, Cleo brought salsa to Spanish class that was so spicy, six students got sick.

True ☐

False ☐

They're all true! How will I ever survive other students knowing she's my sister?

Maybe I can change my last name.

"That's so far away! Don't even think about it. Instead, you should be helping me plan our graduation BBQ. It's all gonna be great!"

"Yeah, great," I said. But I didn't feel so great. Carly's lucky. She has two older brothers who never do anything the least bit annoying or embarrassing. If Cleo were _her_ sister, she'd understand why I'm worried. I tried to explain it at lunch.

I've had two years in a different school from Cleo. I NEED that distance! How can I survive breathing the same high school air as her?

That won't happen until fall!

If you spend all your time worrying about the future, you'll miss out on the _now_.

These are the precious, last golden days of 8th grade!

Even more precious, I thought, because they're Cleo-free. I told Carly I'd stop and smell the daisies, sieze the day, live like there's no tomorrow, whatever cliché she wanted about living in the present. Really I was thinking I needed to count the weeks, the days, the hours, the minutes, the seconds until my world collides with Cleo's.

But to Carly, I just talked about graduation plans.

By the time lunch was over, Carly and I had figured out most of the graduation BBQ details. I'm in charge of junk food and drinks, so as soon as I got home, I left a shopping list on the kitchen counter. We still have a few weeks to go, but I've learned to give Mom a heads-up to avoid the long lectures about irresponsible behavior.

WHAT!?! You need 36 cupcakes by tomorrow morning?!

I HATE IT when you do this to me! Why didn't you tell me you need hundreds of sugar cubes for your California mission project due TOMORROW!?

I can't believe this! You need posterboard NOW? Now?! TONIGHT!?! How long have you known about this assignment?

↑ Mom is just not as prepared or flexible as she should be.

You need WHAT by WHEN?! FORGET IT!!! I've had it!

Unfortunately, Cleo saw the list first. Because she's naturally nosy, another one of her annoying traits.

"Sounds like someone's having a party," she said, sticking her nose solidly where it didn't belong.

"Is this for middle school graduation by any chance?"

I told her it was none of her business. She said it was exactly her business because graduating 8th grade means starting 9th grade, which means high school.

"Which means MY school!" She flashed her evil grin. "We'll be twins!"

"NO! NEVER!" I yelped. Twins?!! I didn't even want to be sisters!

For a second, Cleo actually looked sad.

"You're right," she huffed, back to normal — well, normal for her. "We could never be twins. You'll be a puny, insignificant runt of a freshman and I'll be a glamorous, almost-at-the-top junior." She flounced off and it struck me that I'd hurt her feelings. I even felt a quick twinge of guilt. But no, she couldn't really be glad we'd be in the same school. It had to be an act.

I mean, Cleo's my sister, NOT my friend.

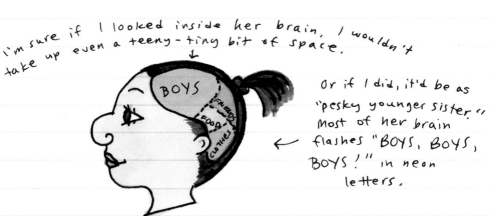

I'm sure if I looked inside her brain, I wouldn't take up even a teeny-tiny bit of space.

BOYS

Or if I did, it'd be as "pesky younger sister." Most of her brain flashes "BOYS, BOYS, BOYS!" in neon letters.

Tonight at dinner, Cleo was still glaring at me. Mom wasn't very nice, either. Did she thank me for my plenty-of advance-warning list? No. Instead, she nagged me about working over the summer. She can't stand the idea of us "rotting our brains out." She doesn't get that's the whole point of summer.

Last summer, I went to camp with Carly — it was great! A wonderful, lazy summer, almost like no camp at all. ↓

We did a whole lot of nothing! ↑

And when Mom says "work," she doesn't mean the kind of jobs I did with Carly. She means summer school, something "academically enriching," which translates into boring.

"Mom, it's my last summer before high school, my last chance to do NOTHING," I pleaded.

"Or you could see it as your first summer before high school, a chance to get ahead," Mom argued.

"I'm going to take a class at community college," Cleo

interrupted Mom's nag and, for once, I was grateful she was there, even though I couldn't imagine Cleo in any kind of college.

But the distraction worked (at first). Mom thought it was a brilliant idea.

I forgot the good part of Cleo being a junior. It means the following year, she'll be a senior. And the year after that, she'll be GONE! Away at college. Unless she ends up living at home, going to community college full-time.

Suddenly, I was eager for her to look amazing on all her applications.

"Have you looked at the University of Alaska? Or Hawaii? Those sound like great places to go," I suggested.

"Say what you really want — for me to go to college on Mars!

Or the Moon!" Cleo snorted.

Mom changed the subject before I could agree.

"While you're taking your class, I have the perfect way for Amelia to spend the summer."

By "perfect," she meant "boring, miserable, awful." I could tell.

"Why don't you go to math camp?"

There were a zillion reasons why NOT! It sounded horrible, so horrible the word "camp" was used instead of "school" to trick you into thinking it might be fun. Kind of like Science Fair, which really has nothing to do with any kind of fair I've ever been to.

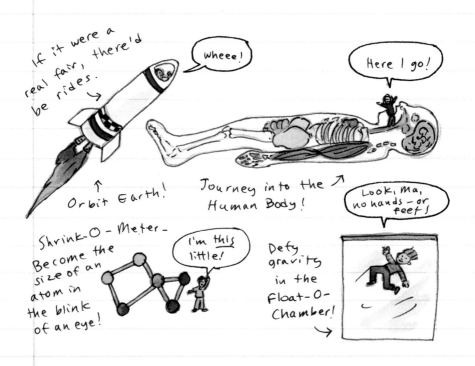

If it were a real fair, there'd be rides. →

wheee!

Here I go!

↑
Orbit Earth!

Journey into the ↗
Human Body!

Look, Ma, no hands - or feet!

Shrink-O-Meter-
Become the size of an atom in the blink of an eye!

I'm this little!

Defy gravity in the Float-O-Chamber! →

There'd be tons of junk food.

↓

Solar-cooked hot dogs!

Invent-a-flavor Ice Slushies – here's botanical blue!

↑

Fried Atoms– you name it, we fry it!

And stupid games with lame prizes.

↓

How cuddly!

Make a complete electrical circuit – win a giant, stuffed battery!

Shoot your rocket the farthest– win a paper airplane!

who took my cheese?

↑

Place bets on the smartest, ~~fastest~~ rat in the maze– win a new pet.

Oof– it's HEAVY!

↑

Guess the density– win a balloon!

But there's none of that stuff at science fairs, just like there's nothing remotely camp-like about Math Camp.

"Well?" Mom asked. As if my answer wasn't obvious. Did she really think I'd say yes?

"I don't need to go! I'm good at math. I get A's." Unlike Cleo who once got a D– (As if a D wasn't bad enough.)

"I just want to be sure you take the harder math classes in high school. Like calculus. I don't want you to be afraid of math." Spoken like the engineer Mom is. She must be disappointed I don't want to follow in her footsteps.

"I'm not afraid of math! I just don't want to waste a summer on it. Especially <u>this</u> summer. I promise I'll take the harder classes. During the school year."

That got Mom to drop the math camp idea, but I knew she'd come up with something else. I had to make plans before she did.

"How about I visit my dad in Chicago?" I suggested. I said "my dad" and not "Dad" because we were never really a family. Not so I'd remember, since he left when I was a bab

Facts about my father
↓

I got to visit him first because I was the one who nagged Mom for his address and wrote to him after so many years without a word. It wasn't easy to get mom to agree — I really wore her down. But I was right — it shouldn't have been such a secret!

↘

I met him three years ago, so obviously I don't know him well. →

And he doesn't know me. When I first saw him, neither of us knew what to say, we ← were both so nervous. I couldn't help noticing how hairy his hands were, but I was polite and shook hands anyway.

He didn't feel ↗ like a dad to me, mostly because I had no idea how that would feel.

And he had this STUPID teddy bear, like he was expecting a baby, not ← me.

He lives in Chicago with his new family — a wife and a little boy named George.
↑

Mom wasn't happy about any of this at first, but she's gotten used to it now. She let Cleo and me go to a big family reunion with Dad and his new family. And she's said before that a summer visit would be okay. So why not this summer?

What about me? It's not fair if Amelia gets a Chicago trip and I don't. Forget about community college! I wanna go too!

↑ Trust Cleo to muck things up! She's still mad that I met Dad first. But I found him!

"Let me talk to your father. We'll figure something out."

So long as there was no more talk of any kind of educational activity for the summer, it was fine with me.

Mom called Dad after dinner, but it wasn't the conversation I expected.

Girls, I'd love to have both of you here for the summer! I was going to call and invite you, but you beat me to it. I have plans for you both, something I'm excited about and I hope you will be too.

I know your mother hasn't raised you as Jews, but I'm Jewish and I'd love for you to be bat-mitzvah'd.

on speaker phone →

I'm sure you have a million questions, but really this is totally possible. You're smart girls, you'll study here over the summer, and then you'll read from the torah. It'll be hard work, but I hope you'll feel it's worthwhile.

My first thought was that if Judaism was so important to Dad, he could have stuck around to give us that. I mean, we could have been raised Jewish.

My second thought was NO STUDYING over the summer. No way! It sounded like I'd have school with Mom, school with Dad. Was there no way out?

Cleo thought it was a great idea.
↓

I've always wanted to be Jewish! I'd love to learn Hebrew! Now I can wear a star of David!

And doesn't a bat mitzvah mean a big party? Plus lots of cash, I mean, presents? Count me in!

This is SO much more important than any class at community college.

↑
I'm sure she thought she'd earn extra points with Dad for doing this, that she'd be his instant favorite. She was probably right, but I was too mad to care.

I thought Mom would be angry, but she agreed with Dad. Maybe she just wanted us both gone for the summer.

I said I'd have to think about it. Dad sounded happy with Cleo, disappointed with me. I'd let down both parents in one evening.

"You don't have to decide right away," Mom said after she'd hung up the phone. "But a bat mitzvah is an important ritual. It marks your becoming a responsible Jewish adult."

"That's asking too much of Amelia. Responsibility? Adulthood? Forget it!" Cleo gloated. She seemed thrilled to be Dad's Jewish daughter. And Mom's responsible one.

The next day at school, I told Carly about Dad and his Instant-Bat-Mitzvah plans.

I know I'm letting him down if I don't do it, but it would be a ton of work. Plus suddenly I have a dad, then suddenly I'm Jewish?

Hey, I'd help you. Maybe you can study here. If you want to, that is.

It was sweet of Carly to offer, but how could she help with Hebrew? I'd have to learn a whole different alphabe (or as Cleo gleefully told me this morning, alefbet — she's already started learning Hebrew with some online progra She's diving right in while I'm hesitating.

I told Carly that what I really wanted was a do-nothing summer. Preferably one with no Cleo around.

I get that! For once my parents said I can have a free summer. No school, camp, work, or community service. Just pool time!

That didn't sound like Carly's mom. at all. Mrs. Tremain was always nagging Carly to learn something or make money. Or do something that would look impressive on college applications, like volunteer at a preschool or a homeless shelter.

"Mom's being nice about this summer," Carly said, as if she could hear my doubts. Still, there was something about the way she said it that made me think her mom wasn't being nice at all.

"Carly, is something else happening?" I know her too well. Something was definitely wrong.

Carly didn't answer, but her face said a lot. →

Whatever it was, it was big, way bigger than my Dad-bat mitzvah problem. ↙

Looking at her, I felt icy cold. "Don't tell me you're moving! Right before high school? Carly, you can't!" I was almost wailing. Actually I _was_ wailing.

"I'm not!" Carly looked ready to cry herself. "We'll still be in the same house."

"Still?" I repeated. "What's happening? Tell me!"

"I wanted to wait until after graduation."

"Why?" I pictured all kinds of terrible scenarios. Carly's mom had cancer or her dad lost his job or one of her brothers was in trouble, like maybe he crashed the car and was in the hospital.

Then in a flash, I knew.

"Your parents are getting divorced? But you'll stay in the same house. You won't have one of those switch-homes-every-other-week deals?"

"No, that's not it. My parents are fine. I'm fine. Everyone's fine."

Except me. I wasn't fine. Because that's when she dropped the bomb on me.

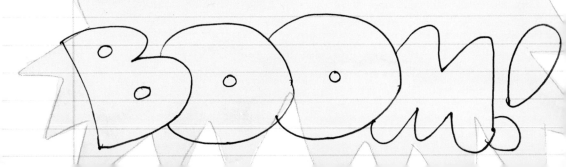

Bomb debris all over the place. ↘

"I'm changing schools."

"We're all changing schools," I said, panicked. "Going from middle school to high school."

Carly sighed. "You know what I mean. I'm going to a private school. I got into Edgewood Prep. My dad says it's easier to get into Stanford or Harvard if I go there. My mom says I need to be more challenged, to work at my full potential."

Harvard!? Stanford!? We were just starting 9th grade!

I couldn't believe Carly's parents were already pressuring her about college. Well, actually, I could, but it seemed so unnecessary and unfair. To her AND to me. How would I survive high school without my best friend?

And if she really was my best friend, why hadn't she told me about any of this? I tried to stay calm on the outside, but on the inside, I was simmering. And terrified.

I didn't feel like a powerful 8th grader anymore, but like a miserable 9th grader. →

Who would I talk to, laugh with, share rumors with?

Whatever tiny bit of coolness I had, I got from Carly. Without her, I'd be a total social loser.

Plus lonely. No more lunch or homework partner.

"What about your brothers?" I asked desperately. "The
go to Oopa High, so why not you?"

My brothers are
the reason I'm going
to prep school. Marcus
didn't get into an ivy
league college and my
parents blame Oopa
High for that.

So now
Malcolm and I
are both going to
Edgewood. That way
we'll both get into
Yale, Stanford,
Harvard, or
Princeton.

That was a crazy reason! Marcus got into UCLA and
U.C. Berkeley. I reminded Carly those were both great
colleges, but she said they weren't good enough for he
parents. They've had their hearts set on the ivies eve
since Carly and her brothers were babies. I guess I'm
lucky they let Carly go to public school at all.

Goo, goo
Stanford!

Goo, goo
Yale!

"The thing is," Carly said, "Malcolm doesn't even want
go to any of those universities. Plus he says it's all way
too much pressure."

My first reaction had been panic, but as we talked, I got angrier and angrier. Until I couldn't hold it in anymore.

"When did all this happen? You took an entrance exam, right? You even toured the stupid prep school, all without saying ANYTHING! TO YOUR BEST FRIEND!!"

I couldn't help it — I could feel how hot my face was. I was furious!

I tell you everything! About my dad, Cleo, mean girls, nice girls, stupid crushes. And you keep this HUGE secret?!

"Calm down, Amelia! I'm sorry, really sorry. I wanted to tell you, but I thought you'd just worry. It seemed better to wait until I knew for sure I got in."

"So when did you find out?"

"Last month," Carly admitted. "And then I didn't want to ruin graduation for you."

"You thought it'd be better to ruin my summer?" I snapped.

"Come on, what was I supposed to do? You know how my parents are. I had to do this and I didn't want to hurt your feelings. It was an impossible situation."

I thought the truth was always possible.

I didn't want to forgive her, but what else could I do? So Carly's not perfect. In this case, she was a total coward.

"Please, Amelia?" Carly pleaded. "Don't make this any harde The pressure to get into a good college is huge."

"Maybe for you." I guess I'm lucky Mom doesn't talk tha much about college. I mean, it's clear Cleo and I will go to one, but all that matters to Mom is that it be affordable (meaning cheap). We'll probably go to a community colleg then transfer to a state school.

Maybe. It hadn't occurred to me that starting high sch meant worrying about getting into a good college. Plus worrying about friends leaving for prep school. I took deep breath and calmed down.

The problem with not being mad anymore was that it le me feeling sad. Sitting in the cafeteria, walking through grimy hallways, I was flooded with nostalgia. We'd face bullies, nasty notes, and tough tests.

I'd thought middle school was hard, but really it was easy. Because Carly had been with me. She said we'd still be best friends, but would we really?

Look what happened with Nadia, my best friend before I moved to Oopa in 4th grade.

when we were little, Nadia and I always made costumes together.

devil

angel

sheep

Bo-p•

kindergarten

3rd grade

We still write letters and visit each other (like last year's disaste but it's not the same. And it won't be the same with Carly.

How can we share jokes about boring teachers and cute boys when we don't know the same people anymore?

I'll have to take the big step of surviving high school without her. Just like Nadia survived middle school without me. Funny, I'd felt she was lucky to stay and it was harder to be the one leaving, but it doesn't feel that way now. Being left behind is no fun. It's hard in its own way.

All of which made this summer more important than ever.

I couldn't go to Chicago, bat mitzvah or no bat mitzvah. I had to stay here, be with Carly. Next year she might not be my friend anymore, at least not the same way as now.

I hated to give Cleo the edge with our dad, but Carly was more important. I'd made my decision.

Carly, I'm not going to Chicago. I want to be with you this summer. Cleo can have my dad all to herself and she can become the big family expert on all things Jewish. I want to relax with you.

"You didn't tell me Cleo's getting bat mitzvah'd too!" Carly burst out laughing. In fact, she laughed so loud and so long, she made me laugh with her. Even though I had no idea what was so funny. She finally explained it:

"I'm just picturing Cleo studying hard. That's like a cow reading or a pig writing poetry!"

I resent that! Cows are much more likely to read!

I love a good sob story! SOB!!

And pigs are fine poets, I'll have you know.

My speciality is haiku.

"You should think about this more. Don't decide yet," Carly said. "Don't you want to spend more time with your dad?"

"Are you trying to get rid of me?" All my anger from before rushed back. Was Carly still my best friend or was she already dumping me for prep school, for all the cool, new friends she'd make?

"Of course not! I'm trying to be a good friend."

"Good friends don't keep secrets, especially not such BIG ones!"

"Amelia, can you let that go? Can we just have fun with our graduation BBQ or are you going to ruin it all?"

That made me even madder! Who was ruining things? She was! But I didn't yell. I didn't scream. I didn't throw things. I just gritted my teeth and said we'd plan more tomorrow.

The end of middle school wasn't turning out to be fun at all. And I certainly didn't feel like celebrating.

That night after dinner, I tried to write a story in my notebook, because usually that helps me figure out what I'm feeling. Sometimes I think I'm furious, but really I'm afraid. Or nervous. Or jealous. This time, though, I just felt angry. Period. It was too wadded up for me to untangle all the different strands.

But for once, I couldn't write anything. I kept thinking of Carly and getting more and more angry.

Then there was a knock on my door. It was Cleo — which was strange because usually she just barges in.

Why were you so upset at dinner? I can tell you're upset because you were so quiet.

What's going on with Cleo? Suddenly, she's so sensitive. I don't get it.

I told her it was none of her business. She said I shouldn't be so hostile.

Hostile? Hostile! Really?!

"What is that?" I snapped. "A vocabulary word for the SAT? Who talks like that?"

"Hostile is a perfectly good word, and you're exemplifying it. 'Exemplify' is an SAT word, if you wanted to know."

Now she was acting like the Cleo I know. Hostile, come to think of it.

"Maybe you'd like to expand your vocabulary and not sound like such an ignoramous, which is another useful SAT word," she sneered.

"Really? It sounds like 'dumb' with a butt attached to it."

"A-mos!" Cleo snarled. "Ig-nor-A-mos!"

"Like I said." I smiled extra-sweetly.

"This is what I get for being nice to you!" Cleo scowled. "I thought you were worried about learning so much Hebrew so quickly. Or that high school worries you. But you're just being a jerk."

For a second, I wondered if I was being mean to Cleo, but then that second was gone.

"So leave me alone," I said. "Don't waste your niceness on me."

"I won't!" huffed Cleo. "And just so you know — you'll be a total loser in high school, the lowest of the low."

Now she was acting like the sister I knew so well. I bet she'd only been nice to me because she wanted to be the expert, to lord her superior status as a junior over me.

I had to admit there were times when Cleo looked out for me. But mostly she was one huge embarrassing pimple, the kind that no amount of make-up can cover.

I did not want to be her twin in high school! →

All of this reminded me that high school meant Cleo school. How would I survive? It was a horrible equation: high school plus Cleo minus Carly equals?

I lay awake a long time.

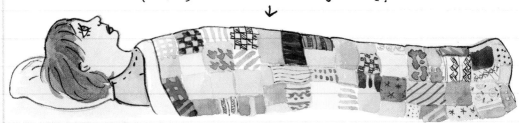

Because each night meant a new day and each day brought me one day closer to the last day of middle school, the last day in school with Carly. And closer to the first day of high school with Cleo.

But first, there were a lot of other "lasts."

Our last oral report together in french class.

Voilà la baguette!*

Voilà, une autre baguette!**

* "Here's the bread!"   ** "Here's another bread!"

Our last time as science partners.
↓

No more shared stories about cafeteria catastrophes. No more joint triumphs doing difficult projects together. No more passing notes or trading gossip.

It was the kind of problem I normally wrote to Nadia about, so I did, even though I'd done the same thing to her.

Dear Nadia,

You know Carly — you met her when you visited and things were bumpy at first, but ended up okay. Anyway, she won't be going to high school with me. She's going to a private prep school instead.

Naturally, I'm worried this will be the end of our friendship. Plus I'll have to face high school without a best friend!

I know you have experience with this from when I moved away. Now I have a better sense of what you felt like then (and I'm SO sorry).

So what should I do? Yours till the pencil tips, amelia

I felt better just writing to Nadia. At least that still worked for me. And I decided to do something, not just mope. I invited Carly to sleep over on Friday night. Summer hasn't even started yet, but I couldn't help wondering if this would be my last sleep-over with her. Yet another last thing.

As part of her new Jewish studies, Cleo insisted on practicing Friday night prayers. →

Meaning, lighting candles, drinking wine, eating a special bread, all with prayers first. Cleo's so gung-ho about all this Jewish stuff — it's weird were WEIRD!

we could only eat after all 3 prayers were said. And I thought Judaism was all about food!

challah →

mom let us have just a sip of wine, but the best part was the bread — it was delicious

Worst of all was Cleo's know-it-all attitude. She said she was supposed to wear a beanie to say the prayers, but since she didn't have one — yet, she insisted — she wore a stupid baseball cap. Mom said they're not called beanies anyway. They're kippot or yamakas → (I'm not sure how to spell these things). Is everyone suddenly an expert on Jewish stuff except me?

Mom had a fake smile plastered on her face, like she wanted to be supportive, but didn't really mean it. That made me think it was a good time to tell her my decision. I thought she'd be relieved I didn't want to visit Dad after all, that I didn't want to be bat mitzvah'd. But she wasn't. She just said we'd talk about it later.

Cleo, though, was thrilled.

"I'm not surprised," she gloated. "Why be part of a ritual marking how mature you are when you're still such a baby?"

"Am not!" I said.

"Are too!" she said.

we showed just how grown-up ← we could be. →

Mom said to stop it, and Carly looked embarrassed. If she was really my friend, she'd take my side. But she acted like a polite guest and didn't say anything until we were back in my room after dinner. Then, instead of saying how horrible Cleo was, she said I should really think about the bat mitzvah. As if I hadn't already.

"Learning about your roots could be interesting. It could be important for you," she argued. "Cleo's really into it."

"That's a reason against the whole Jewish discovery trip, not for it. Besides, what about you?"

"What about me?" she asked, but she knew what I meant.

"We might not be friends once you're in a different high school." There, I'd said it.

"We'll still be friends. Maybe not eating-lunch-together friends, but still friends." Carly got quiet. "It'll be lonely without you."

I'd been so busy worrying about myself, I hadn't thought what it would be like for Carly.

"Are you scared? Nervous? Worried?" I asked.

"A little bit of all three. Plus excited. Maybe it'll be fun. I can take classes there that don't exist at Oopa High, like Russian or Art History."

Those weren't selling points for me, but I was glad they made Carly happy.

She fell asleep right away, but I watched her for a while, wondering what she would be like at the <u>end</u> of high school. She'd be great, that's for sure, but would she still be my friend?

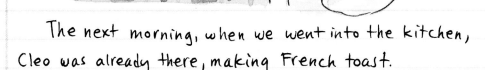

The next morning, when we went into the kitchen, Cleo was already there, making French toast.

Why are you up so early?

Why are you?

This isn't early for me, but it is for you.

If you must know, I'm working today. I got a job at the mall.

Really? Since when?

Since last week. I work in a bookstore — it's the best job ever!

I felt a quick stab of jealousy. That was the perfect job for <u>me</u> — being around books all day, getting to read new, fresh-baked stories.

"Congratulations, Cleo," Carly said. "You must be excited — about that <u>and</u> the bat mitzvah plans."

"I am!" Cleo grinned proudly. "Almost as excited as I am about my little sister and her little best friend (she winked at Carly in case she didn't know who that was) "being in my same school."

Carly looked at me, then back at Cleo.

"I guess Amelia hasn't mentioned it yet. I'm going to Edgewood Prep School, not Oopa High."

Cleo looked genuinely shocked and hurt. As if it was <u>her</u> best friend deserting her, not mine.

Why are you going to such a snooty place? Everyone there is super-rich and super-stuck up.

I felt worse than ever.
What kind of friend was I?
It sounded way harder for Carly
to go to a snooty new school where she didn't know anyone
than for me to go to Oopa High without her.

After all, I'd be with kids I'd known since middle school. Leah would be there. And Maya. And a sea of familiar faces.

↑ the girl I wanted to be just like until I realized I didn't   ↑ the girl who shared lunch with me once   ↑ the boy I did a science project with   ↑ the boy I had a crush on   ↑ the mean girl who p... nasty not... in my loc...

But Carly just said, "It won't be like that."

"I hope for your sake, it isn't," Cleo said. "And remember you can always transfer back."

After Cleo left, holding her plate piled high with French toast, I told Carly I was sorry and she shouldn't pay attention to anything Cleo said. She wasn't an expert on prep school. What did she know?

Actually, she's kinda right.

But there are regular kids like me there, too. Not just rich spoiled brats.

Malcolm says there are good people wherever you go. You just have to find them.

But I won't find another friend like you.

"You won't need to," I said. "You'll still have me as a friend." And she'd make plenty of new ones. Carly was good at fitting in anywhere. If I could handle the move to Oopa, she could deal with the move to Edgewood Prep. I told her how nervous and worried I was when I first came here. I even showed her the notebook I started then, full of all my fears.

That's when I first kept a notebook. Mom thought writing down my thoughts and feelings would make the move easier. →

I didn't believe her, but it turned out, she was right. ↙

"Wow!" said Carly. "So moving is what turned you into a writer and an artist."

I hadn't thought of it like that, but yeah, that was true.

"So what will going to Edgewood do for me?" Carly wondered. "Maybe I should start my own journal."

I thought that was a great idea. Plus I had to admit, I loved the idea of Carly following in my footsteps. It made me feel proud.

That was it, though, for talk about high school. We spent the rest of the day finalizing plans for the Graduation BBQ Celebration Extravaganza. The big finale would be a treasure hunt.

treasure
chest
(made from
papier maché?)
→

I love treasure
hunts!
↙

Nobody can be
sad or worried while
looking for — and finding
treasure!

We decided to make it really complicated. We'll divide everyone into two teams, racing against each other, th working together. We'll start them off with a riddle.

Each riddle will lead to another riddle-clue and puzzle piece. When all the puzzle pieces have been found, then the teams have to work together to ma the puzzle. The puzzle will show them a map, and the map will have an X, which marks the spot, lea them to the treasure.

Pretty cool, huh?

Carly assigned me to choose the prizes for inside the chest, so now I have to figure out something extra-special. I want to really surprise Carly.

One surprise will be that the treasure chest will be a piñata, because those are easy to find.

So whatever's inside has to withstand a beating.

← or I guess we could cut it open instead.

Real pirate chests are impossible to find.

After Carly went home, I tried to come up with something amazing. So far, nothing.

I was so desperate, I even asked Cleo for her advice when she got back from her bookstore job.

"Remember your first year in high school? What do you wish you'd had then? What would have been most useful?"

I thought she'd say a better personality.

Better clothes.

Better make-up.

"Besides stuff that has to do with your looks," I said. "M
friends aren't like that."

"Everyone's like that," Cleo said flatly. "Anyone who
says they don't want to be pretty is lying. It's just hum
nature."

I had to admit she was right — not that I'd tell her th
Of course, I want to be pretty. But I also want to be a g
artist and writer.

"There are psychological studies that show how attracti
people get better jobs and are paid more. It's a fact," Cl
argued.

"Maybe. But that's not what this BBQ is about. We'r
celebrating the end of middle school and the start of h
school. So I want the prizes to be a kind of welcome to
grade thing."

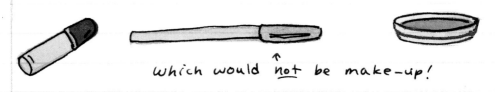

which would not be make-up!

"It's also a good-bye party for Carly," Cleo said. Was sh
being sensitive again? Maybe the whole Jewish studie
thing was actually turning her into a responsible adult,
the way it's supposed to. Whatever it was, this was a
new, improved Cleo. Plus she'd given me a great idea,

Now I knew what the treasure should be. And I had a lot of work to do.

But first the mail came — with a postcard from Nadia!

Dear Amelia,
I could see what a great friend Carly is when I was there, so I don't think you have anything to worry about. True, you won't be in the same classes, but that could happen even in the same high school. At least you still live close by, so you can do stuff outside of school. You just have to take care of the friendship, water it like a plant, so it doesn't dry up. Yours 'til the flower gardens. Nadia

Amelia
564 N. Hamerest
Oopa, OR
97881

↖ Old-fashioned letters are still the best!

Nadia had a point. You shouldn't take friends for granted, close by or far away. I could still be best friends with Carly. I'd just have to work at it more.

The last days of school, I tried hard to be a perfect friend. I didn't mention high school at all. Everyone was too excited about graduation, about a long summer of freedom, to think about next fall.

Yearbooks were passed out, full of embarrassing photos.

That was a sign that any attempt at education was officially over. Classes meant parties, passing around yearbooks for signing, and watching movies. Tests were over. We were all just waiting for the last day to finally come, teachers as much as students.

Mom says yearbooks are an expensive waste of money, so I decided to make my own yearbook for friends to sign. Now this is a combination notebook-yearbook, which makes sense since it's already full of middle-school nostalgia. Only instead of embarrassing photos, there are embarrassing drawings.

Instead of photos of the debate team or football games, I'm including the real lessons I learned in middle school.

① How Gossip Works and How to Handle it:

Ⓐ Pretend that you have <u>no</u> idea there's a horrible rumor about you.

> You're asking if I've heard about the disgusting gym locker?

> And how I what? No, nope, not a word.

Ⓑ Act like you know even juicier gossip.

> That rumor about me is nothing compared to the one I heard. Nope, sorry, I can't tell you — it's WAY too explosive!

Ⓒ Exaggerate the rumor to make it so ridiculous, it's unbelievable.

> Yeah, of course I did!

> Not only did I break into the principal's office, I used my amazing skills to change everyone's grades, ages, and names on the computer.

The Gossip Ripple Effect
↓

The circle of kids who know the cool kids hear about it next.

Rumor starts here.

Immediately, all the cool, in-the-know kids pick up on it.

This is a bigger group, so the rumor spreads faster.

The outcasts nobody likes or talks to know the rumor by now. They're the last to hear it.

The kids who aren't popular, but aren't unpopular either, are the biggest group of all. Once they hear it, it's all over the place — nothing can stop the spread of it now.

But once they do — the rumor is EVERYWHERE!

More stuff I learned in middle school.

How _not_ to handle a huge backpack.
↓

Don't let this happen to you!
↓

I can't get up!

Help! I'm crushed by school supplies.

Instead of feeling like a cool, big kid, I felt like a bug being squashed.

Worse, if you lose your balance and tip over, you're done for. You'll never get up!

Plus, of course, lots of stuff about boys.
↓

The Truth Behind Boy and Girl Things: circle all the answers that fit.

To make a product for girls, you add:
(a) pink or purple   (b) lace or ribbons   (c) bows
(d) eyelashes   (e) flowers or hearts   (f) ponies

To make a product for boys:
(a) lightning bolts   (b) camouflage colors   (c) blue
(d) guns or knives   (e) race cars

Correct answer: none of the above. Those are what stupid corporations **think** boys and girls like. They're wrong! All girls aren't the same and neither are all boys. So even if a lot girls like pink, I don't have to like it, too.

Middle school also taught me about school dances.

what always happens
↓

① Someone will spill a drink on someone else.

Hey!

Oops!

Sorry!

② A toilet will get clogged and overflow.

③ A teacher will tell a lame joke.

Have you heard the one about the potato and the carrot?

④ Palms will get sweaty, armpits will get itchy, every pimple will look three times worse than normal.

Ugh!

⑤ A song everyone hates will be played and booed at.

BOOO!   HISS!   YUCCH!

I know yearbooks feature clubs and sports and dances, plus everyone's picture. But my yearbook has the stuff that mattered most to me. I learned how to handle mean girls and oral reports, friends fighting and crushes on boys. I got better at writing and drawing. That's all stuff I'll bring with me to high school, even without Carly being there.

And to make this a real yearbook (it's already a real notebook), I'm using the last pages for kids to sign. Some people are really picky (or snobby?) and only want close friends to write in their yearbooks, but I don't care. I want as many signatures as possible. Besides, I figure that if I ask people to sign my yearbook-notebook, they'll ask me to sign theirs. And signing other kids' yearbooks is just as important as getting signatures. They're both marks of popularity. Which normally I wouldn't care about, but this was my last chance for a teeny, tiny bit of middle-school coolness.

Finally, finally, <u>FINALLY</u> it was G Day – Graduation Day, the last official day of middle school!

The girls wore nice dresses. The boys had on button-down shirts, nice pants (no jeans allowed!), and sometimes even suit jackets.

Everyone looked fancy. And hot. And bored. Add itchiness for me since I had to wear a stupid hand-me-down dress of Cleo's. I <u>hate</u> being the younger sister. The only new things I get are shoes, socks, and underwear (thank goodness!).

I thought graduation would be fun, but it was long, sweaty, and dull, full of mind-numbing speeches. I counted how many times people used the word "special." 26 times! That didn't sound special at all.

Such a special day...

Not to mention the special achievements...

This class is special...

A special time in your lives... full of special people... special memories...

Today's cafeteria special is tacos...

And for those with special needs...

... a time of special pet peeves about the use of "special."

Just as my eyes were starting to glaze over from all the sugary specialness, something happened that woke me up. It was even – dare I say it? – special.

The principal was droning on about some student who had excellent grades, amazing test scores...

...plus was active in student government and helped with all kinds of extra-curricular projects. Sounded like exactly the kind of person I'd hate for being so perfect,

In fact, this student is so special, she deserves the Principal's Award for this year. So it is with tremendous pride and appreciation that I give this honor to...

"CARLY TREMAIN!"

I was so excited, I stood up, clapping and cheering.
And like a wave, all these other kids followed me. Carly
walked up to get her plaque, and we all yelled like
crazy people.

Carly looked surprised and happy and proud and
excited, all at once. For a second, I thought maybe now
her parents would let her go to Oopa High because
Carly's a star in public school and truly appreciated.

But knowing Mr. and Mrs. Tremain, I doubt it.

I hugged Carly before she sat down again.

"Congratulations!" I whispered into her ear. "You so
deserve this!"

It was the best moment in the whole graduation.
After that, I didn't even care how boring and pointless
all the stupid "special" speeches were.

I just sat next to Carly, staring at the plaque in her lap, feeling the waves of happiness radiating out of her.

dazed, smiling Carly →

me, as proud as could be ←

I forgot all about the dumb itchy dress. ←

If she had to go to another school, at least she was leaving this one on a high note. Her award made all the blah blah blahness yakkity shmakkity worth it.

Then it was over – OVER! People were hugging and screaming. We were free, free of middle school forever! I know graduation isn't a "special" achievement (despite all the stupid speeches). After all, everyone finishes middle school. (Don't you have to? Isn't it the law?) But I was still plenty happy to be done with it all, and so was everyone else.

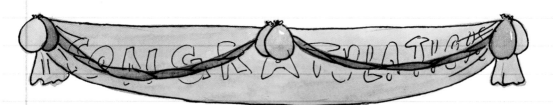

Mom and Cleo came over to congratulate me, and Mom explained for the hundredth time why Dad hadn't come. It's not as if I expected him to. Like I said, who doesn't graduate from middle school? I knew he planned to see me and Cleo soon for our bat mitzvah studies. I told him I'm staying, but he's sure I'll change my mind. So is Mom. Dad doesn't know how stubborn I am, but Mom does. She should know better.

Cleo waited until Mom started talking to another parent. Then she gave me this envelope. ↙

Wrapped in a ribbon to look extra-gifty. →

I was so surprised, I almost dropped it. ←

"Look," she said, "I know it can be hard being my sister. I'm a tough act to follow. But I can also be a help."

She didn't wait for me to say thank you or open it, just left me there with my mouth hanging open.

Who _was_ that person? Cleo? Really? I tore open the envelope, figuring it was some kind of joke present. Like a tee shirt. But it wasn't. It was a map, a really cool one.

I'm with stupid →

hand-drawn and labeled →

← Ooo
Hig

Besides marking shortcuts so you could get to class on time even during the shortest passing periods, it showed the best vending machines, the least smelly parts of the cafeteria, the gym lockers to avoid, along with a list of the easiest, most fun electives and the worst, avoid-at-all-costs teachers. It was a real treasure map!

Maybe I was wrong about Cleo. Maybe it would be useful having her in the same school. So long as nobody knew we were related.

I couldn't wait to show Carly. Her family was heading for the refreshment table (where Mom and Cleo were already busy). She gave her brothers another hug, then came over to see what I was holding.

Carly had a real reason to be congratulated with her amazing award.

Her parents were beaming and so were her brothers. You could see how proud of her they were.

"Did you get an award, too?" she asked. "for best artist?"
"Not an award, but something almost as good."

I unfolded the map. "Don't you wish you could use this with me? It's like a secret guide to Oopa High."

Carly grinned. "Did Cleo make this for you? I'm glad she's looking out for you." She linked her arm in mine. "Now let's say good-bye to this place."

The school was so full of excitement, I thought I might actually miss it. But then we walked past the Bathroom-Nobody-Dares-Enter-Due-to-Never-Flushing-Always-Full-Toilets, and I thought, "Naaaah."

Still the official graduation party was fun, not just another lame school dance. Even if (especially if) you didn't dance, there were fun things to do.

like pose for silly photos →

Oink! ←

The <u>real</u> celebration, though, was the next day, our BBQ. I went over to Carly's early to help set up.

We hid the clues to the treasure hunt.
↓

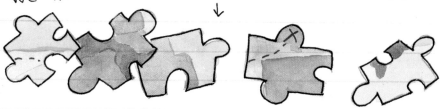

Carly wanted to know what I'd ended up choosing for the treasure. I told her it was a surprise, even for her. "After all, you've done most of the work," I said, "Don't you deserve a little mystery?"

See? That's why we'll always be friends! You do these kinds of things for me. You think of them.

Carly looked really happy — and she didn't even know what the treasure was! →

Carly's brothers did all the grilling. There were hot dogs, hamburgers, veggie burgers. It was a real feast!

Plus Maya brought watermelon. ↙

Leah made potato salad. ↘

Everyone brought something. There was so much food, it felt like a major occasion. And really, it was. It was the end of middle school, the start of high school, my last classes with Carly, my first back in the same school as Cleo, plus the first of Carly's many achievements.

I bet she wins tons of awards.

Nobody used the word "special" once, but we all had a great time. We toasted ourselves with root beer, with an extra toast for Carly — and for her brothers' superior BBQ skills. We played silly games like Twister, Celebrity, and Charades. Then it was time for the treasure hunt.

Clue #1 for the blue team ↓

I'm coiled like a snake, but instead of hissing, I go splishing.

Clue #1 for the red (okay, pink) team ↓

My job is simple — to let people walk all over me. Boring!!

Carly and I gave hints when people got stuck, but that didn't happen much. Soon the two teams had found all the puzzle pieces and put together the map.

Which led them right to the treasure chest.

hidden between the recycling bins in the garage

"What a great idea," Carly said. "A treasure chest piñata! Let's string it up and crack it open."

"No, wait," I said. "This piñata isn't full of candy. Whacking it will break the treasure, so it has to be untaped and cut open. Carly, you do the honors."

I had a kitchen knife handy for her to use.

While Carly carefully sliced, everyone started clapping and chanting.

piñata scraps ↓

Maybe Carly thought the chant was because of her award, but when I'd decided on the treasure, I hadn't even known about that. That made the surprise extra-surprising.

"You wrapped the prizes like presents?" Carly smiled. "Cool!" She picked one and handed it to Leah.

"It's not for me," said Leah. "Look at the card."

"Oh, I didn't realize the prizes were personalized."
Carly picked up another package. "Let's see who this
one is for.

She tried another package.

Carly stopped, dazed for the second time. "Are they
all for me? Why? What's going on?"
"Because," I said, "this isn't just a graduation BBQ.
This is a good-bye and good-luck-at-Edgewood-
Prep party for you!"

"To Carly!" I cheered. "And her success in high school and afterwards!"

"To Carly!!!" Everyone yelled.

Carly looked like she was going to cry.

You guys!

You're the best!

But really, she was very, very happy.

We had each chosen something special for Carly (there's that word again!). I mean something we thought would mean a lot to her. Leah had made her a charm bracelet. Maya got her a beautiful fountain pen with ink in fancy, wax-sealed bottles.

My fingers were itching to draw with it.

Danesha gave her a set of nail polish, all different colors.

They looked delicious! ↗

But since Carly's my best, best, BEST friend, I had two presents for her.

The first was a necklace with a chai, the Hebrew word for life (like in the toast, "l'chaim!" Not like the Indian tea). I told her I might not be getting bat mitzvah'd (yet), but I still wanted to learn about Judaism. Jewelry seemed a good place to start.

Chai necklace ↗

"I hope when you wear this, you'll be having fun in your new life, in your new school, with new friends, but that you'll still remember your old life and your old friends. Like me."

← Believe it or not, Cleo helped me pick out the necklace at a Judaica store. She's becoming quite the expert on all this stuff. She told me what chai means. And then she bought a necklace like this for me. I thought that was my graduation present, not the map.

The new, improved Cleo,
at least sometimes. ↑

The second present was a yearbook, really a yearsbook - a book I'd made for her of all our years together.

I put in photos, drawings, recipes, ticket stubs, campaign flyers, business cards, comic book pages. It was a record of all the things we'd done together. And then I'd had all our friends sign the back pages, just like a real yearbook, so everyone could share their memories.

I know high school will be different, a whole new set of challenges. Maybe like middle school^2 (middle school squared). And I won't have Carly to face it all with me. But she's still my friend. She'll always be my friend.

I've done this before, faced a new school, a new place, strange teachers with strange rules,

I've done it all before and I'll do it all again — face changes, both good and bad. Whatever happens, one thing's for sure - I'll write and draw about all of it. Because pens and paper can be good friends, too.

After all, I've made notebooks since 4th grade, all through middle school. Why not in high school? Writing always helps me figure things out. Cleo's map is a big help (even if Cleo herself isn't always), but I'll still need friends. And a notebook.

So this is the end of middle school

and the end of this notebook...

... and maybe the beginning of another one.

NO PEEKING! THIS MEANS YOU, CLEO!

Amelia's 8th Grade Yearbook
SIGNATURE PAGES
SIGN HERE
↓

To Amelia—
the best BEST BEST
friend ever — may you keep
on writing and drawing always.
I can't wait to see what you
write about next!
xoxoxo Carlos (forever!)

AMELIA—
REMEMBER
WHEN YOU BAKED
THOSE COOKIES
FOR MR. LAMBAS?
HA HA! DON'T TRY
THAT IN HIGH
SCHOOL!
MAYA

Amelia—
See you
in art class in
9th grade! I hear
they have real, live models
to draw from — I can't wait!
Leah

Hey, Amelia—
I plan on
sleeping late ALL
summer. Hope you
do, too. We'll wake
up in 9th grade.
Felix

Amelia—Let's start
with a clean page in
high school. Friends?!
I hope so! Sadie

Amelia—
Here's to NO embarrassing moments
in high school. Fingers —and toes—crossed!
Sharleen